I Have
Chicken Pox

Gillian Gosman

PowerKiDS
press

New York

Published in 2013 by The Rosen Publishing Group, Inc.
29 East 21st Street, New York, NY 10010

First Edition

Editor: Jennifer Way
Book Design: Greg Tucker
Layout Design: Kate Laczynski

Photo Credits: Cover Digital Vision/Getty Images; pp. 4–5, 7 iStockphoto/Thinkstock; p. 6 Mieke Dalle/Photographer's Choice/Getty Images; p. 8 © www.iStockphoto.com/Bojan Fatur; p. 9 George Musil/Visuals Unlimited/Getty Images; p. 10 Goodshoot/Thinkstock; p. 11 Hemera/Thinkstock; p. 12 VStock/Thinkstock; p. 13 Thinkstock/Comstock/Thinkstock; pp. 14, 22 Comstock Images/Comstock/Thinkstock; p. 15 © www.iStockphoto.com/Diana Ponikvar; p. 16 Jupiterimages/Goodshoot/Thinkstock; p. 17 Ken Cavanagh/Photo Researchers/Getty Images; p. 18 Ross Whitaker/The Image Bank/Getty Images; p. 19 (top) Rubberball/Nicole Hill/Getty Images; p. 19 (bottom) John Block/Botanica/Getty Images; p. 20 Shutterstock.com; p. 21 Wavebreak Media/Thinkstock.

Library of Congress Cataloging-in-Publication Data

Gosman, Gillian.
 I have chicken pox / by Gillian Gosman. — 1st ed.
    p. cm. — (Get well soon!)
 Includes index.
 ISBN 978-1-4488-7411-8 (library binding)
 1. Chickenpox—Juvenile literature. I. Title.

RC125.G68 2013
616.9'14—dc23

2011049712

Manufactured in the United States of America

CPSIA Compliance Information: Batch #SW12PK: For Further Information contact Rosen Publishing, New York, New York at 1-800-237-9932

Contents

I Have Chicken Pox

When your parents were children, almost every child scratched his way through a case of chicken pox. At first, he may have felt like he was coming down with the flu. Then he would have seen the first itchy, red **blisters** break out on his skin. He could not keep from scratching those blisters. Then he saw more and more blisters appear. He knew he had come down with chicken pox!

Today, chicken pox is much less common. Young people can still catch it, though. It is important to know what it is, how this **contagious** illness spreads, and how to treat it.

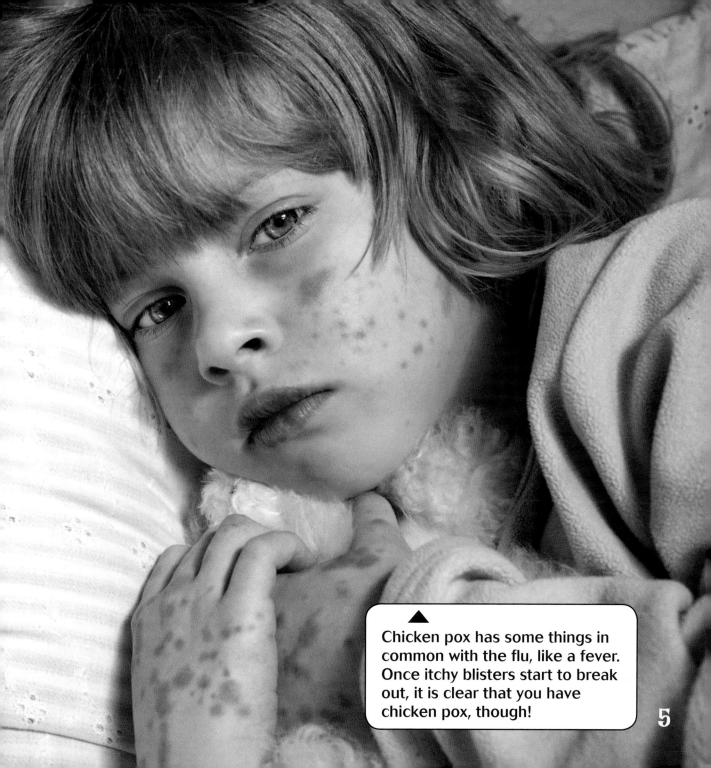

Chicken pox has some things in common with the flu, like a fever. Once itchy blisters start to break out, it is clear that you have chicken pox, though!

5

What Is Chicken Pox?

Staying home and resting when you have chicken pox will help you get better faster and keep you from spreading germs to others. ▼

A **virus** causes chicken pox. It is best known by the small, round blisters that spread across the body of an **infected** patient. It can also cause many of the same **symptoms** that usually come with a case of another common virus called the flu. These include body aches, fevers, headaches, and stomachaches.

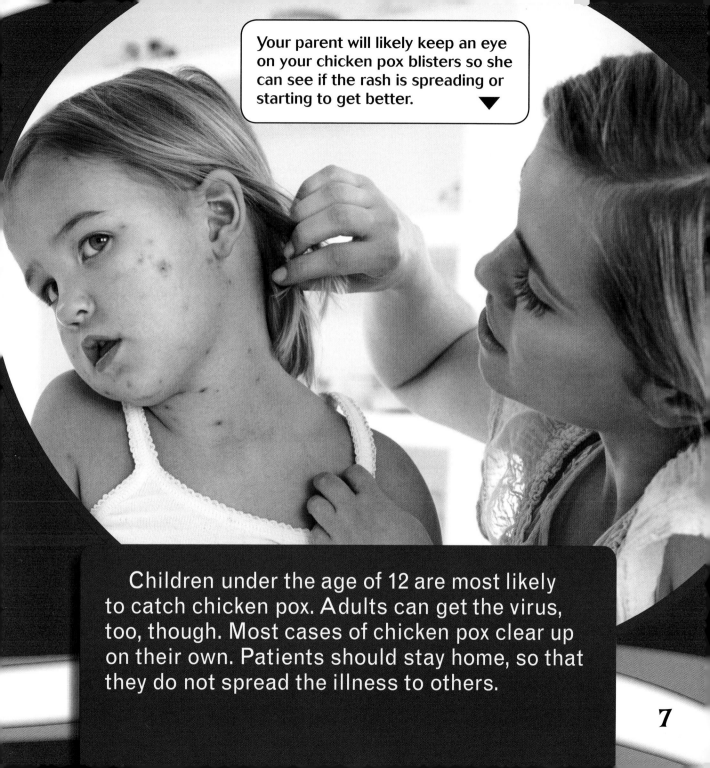

Your parent will likely keep an eye on your chicken pox blisters so she can see if the rash is spreading or starting to get better. ▼

Children under the age of 12 are most likely to catch chicken pox. Adults can get the virus, too, though. Most cases of chicken pox clear up on their own. Patients should stay home, so that they do not spread the illness to others.

What Causes Chicken Pox?

Chicken pox is caused by the varicella-zoster virus. It is called VZV, too. A virus is much too small to be seen by the human eye alone. It must take over a healthy host, or a living thing that carries it. It cannot be on its own.

Chances are good that your body will be host to many viruses throughout your life.

You will likely start to feel better before your chicken pox blisters are completely healed. You may feel better, but you are still contagious!

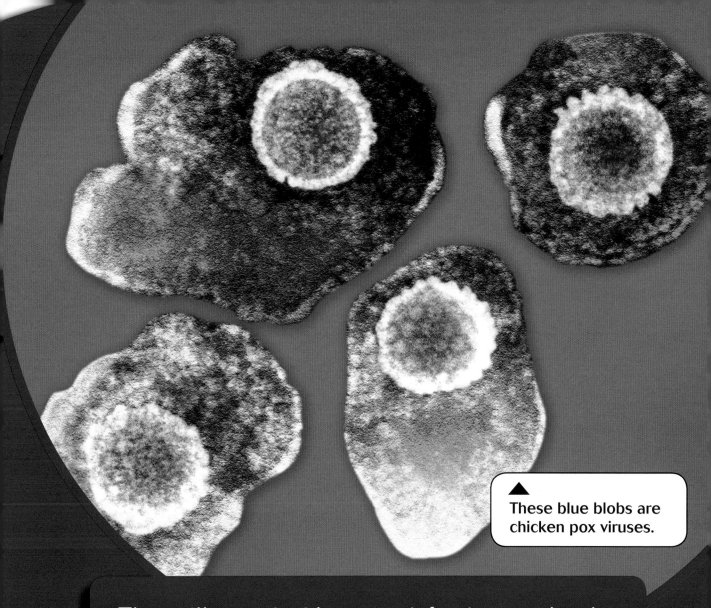

These blue blobs are chicken pox viruses.

They will come inside, cause infections, and make you feel terrible. Fortunately, your body has an **immune system** that fights viruses and other germs. When this happens, you start to get better.

Signs and Symptoms

Feeling tired or having a headache are symptoms you may have when you are sick. ▼

When you are sick, you experience both **signs** and symptoms. A sign is the information a doctor can gather by looking or using medical tools. A symptom is a medical term for the information that you tell a doctor about what and how you are feeling.

The first symptoms of chicken pox include a fever and headache. When signs like blisters appear, the diagnosis is clear. Blisters usually appear first on the patient's back and face. Then they spread to the rest of the body. Most patients have hundreds of blisters!

▲
Here is a close-up shot of chicken pox blisters. This rash is a sign of chicken pox. Doctors can test the liquid in the blisters to make sure it is chicken pox.

What's Going On in My Body?

Like all viruses, chicken pox enters the body, finds a healthy **cell**, and takes over. The virus then makes copies of itself inside the cell. It stretches the cell wall until it bursts. This releases the copied viruses, which move on to other healthy cells. As the virus spreads, you start to feel sick and your

When your immune system is fighting an infection, you often run a fever.

When you have chicken pox, your parent might cut your nails to keep you from scratching and hurting your skin.

skin starts breaking out in a blistery rash. This is when your body's immune system kicks into high gear. All of your body's energy goes toward fighting the chicken pox virus. This is why you often feel worn out when you are sick.

How Did I Catch Chicken Pox?

It is important to use tissues and cover your nose and mouth when you cough or sneeze to keep from spreading germs. ▼

Viruses travel from a sick person to a healthy person in the form of **mucus**. This is the gooey liquid in your nose, mouth, and throat. When a person coughs or sneezes, his mucus, and any germs in it, are released into the air. The mucus might land on another person or on a surface that is soon touched by another person. This is one way you can catch chicken pox.

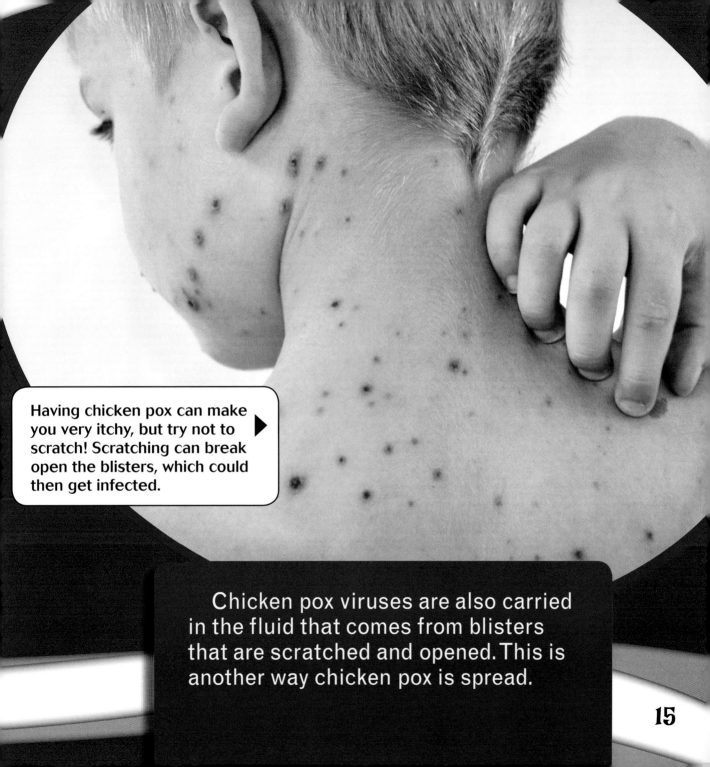

Having chicken pox can make you very itchy, but try not to scratch! Scratching can break open the blisters, which could then get infected.

Chicken pox viruses are also carried in the fluid that comes from blisters that are scratched and opened. This is another way chicken pox is spread.

Going to the Doctor

Because chicken pox is caused by a virus, there is no **prescription** medicine to treat the illness. You just have to let chicken pox run its course. However, you can treat the itchy rash with over-the-counter creams or medicines.

You should go to the doctor right away if you have a high fever that lasts several days, if your

The doctor will ask you about your symptoms and look for signs of other illnesses.

Calamine lotion soothes itchy skin. Your doctor might suggest your parent put some on your chicken pox blisters. ▼

neck feels stiff, if you have a hard time breathing, or if green or yellow **pus** comes from your blisters. These could be signs and symptoms of more serious illnesses.

How Chicken Pox Is Treated

A cool bath can soothe your itchy rash. This will help keep you from wanting to scratch it! ▼

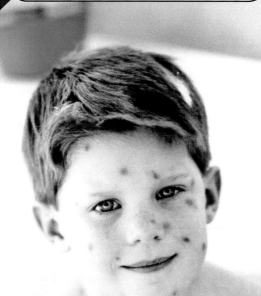

The best way to treat chicken pox is to make yourself feel comfortable. If you are comfortable, you are less likely to scratch your blisters, which could open them and put you at risk of getting a more serious infection.

You could take cool baths and use soothing lotions on your skin. Your parent can give you an over-the-counter pain reliever if you have a fever

Soaps that have oatmeal in them can calm your itchy skin. Your parents might also use calamine lotion or over-the-counter anti-itch creams on your rash.

▲ Some parents put gloves on their kids' hands so they do not scratch their chicken pox rash in their sleep.

or headache. You should stay home from school while you are contagious. You will be contagious until all of your blisters have dried up. This usually takes about one week.

How to Prevent Chicken Pox

You likely got the chicken pox **vaccine** when you were a baby and again when you were four to six years old. The vaccine is a shot that helps give you **immunity** to chicken pox. Vaccination is not 100 percent effective. If you have been vaccinated and get chicken pox, you will likely have a very mild case, though.

◀ Cleaning kitchen counters, tables, and other shared surfaces helps keep the chicken pox virus and other germs from spreading.

Studies show that the chicken pox vaccine is between 80 and 90 percent effective in preventing chicken pox.

To keep from getting chicken pox, you should avoid people who are sick with it. Washing your hands in warm, soapy water and cleaning shared surfaces help stop the spread of chicken pox viruses and other germs.

The Road to Recovery

Your chicken pox blisters will likely clear up in about a week. When they do, you will no longer be contagious, so you can go back to school. ▼

After you have had chicken pox, you will carry the chicken pox virus with you for the rest of your life. In some adults, the chicken pox virus returns in the form of shingles. Shingles is a painful rash that appears on the skin of a patient when she is under stress and the immune system is weak.

Chicken pox is no fun, but for most kids it usually goes away within a week. Now you know what happens if you get chicken pox and how to take care of yourself so you make a speedy recovery!

Glossary

blisters (BLIS-turz) Sore places that look like bubbles on the skin.

cell (SEL) The basic unit of living things.

contagious (kun-TAY-jus) Can be passed on.

immune system (ih-MYOON SIS-tem) The system that keeps the body safe from sicknesses.

immunity (ih-MYOO-nuh-tee) The ability to resist infection by a particular disease.

infected (in-FEK-ted) Became sick from germs.

mucus (MYOO-kus) Thick, slimy matter produced by the bodies of many animals.

prescription (prih-SKRIP-shun) A drug that a doctor orders for a patient who is sick.

pus (PUS) Thick liquid that comes from an infection.

signs (SYNZ) Things that show that one might have an illness.

symptoms (SIMP-tumz) Information patients give doctors about illnesses based on what they are feeling.

vaccine (vak-SEEN) A shot that keeps a person from getting a certain sickness.

virus (VY-rus) Something tiny that causes a disease.

Index

Websites

Due to the changing nature of Internet links, PowerKids Press has developed an online list of websites related to the subject of this book. This site is updated regularly. Please use this link to access the list: www.powerkidslinks.com/gws/pox/

24